W9-BTT-769

For ~~Abby~~ Abigal
A fairy house fan
who has spread the joy
of fairy houses!

FOREST SECRETS

A Fairy Houses Mystery

Explore your creative
Talents!
So great to see you
Tracy Kane
2015

and katelyn
Rice ♡

FOREST SECRETS

A Fairy Houses Mystery

by
Tracy Kane
and **Kelly Sanders**

Light-Beams
PUBLISHING
Lee, New Hampshire

Author/Illustrator: Tracy Kane
Author: Kelly Sanders
Design: Barry Kane
Art Director/Design: Tracy Kane

Publisher's Cataloging-In-Publication Data
(Prepared by The Donohue Group, Inc.)

Kane, Tracy L.
   Forest secrets : a fairy houses mystery / by Tracy Kane and Kelly Sanders.
-- 1st ed.

   p. : ill. ; cm. -- (The fairy houses series ; 7)

   Summary: Kate and Luke find a hidden fairy house in the woods with a
clue inside. Determined to solve the mystery, they discover the wonders of the
forest, only to find it is threatened by development.
   ISBN: 978-0-9766289-1-0

1. Fairies--Juvenile fiction. 2. Natural resources--Conservation and
preservation--Juvenile fiction. 3. Friendship--Juvenile fiction. 4. Fairies--
Fiction. 5. Forests--Fiction. 6. Friendship--Fiction. 7. Mystery fiction. I.
Sanders, Kelly. II. Title.

PZ7.K12757 For 2009
[Fic]   2009924826

13 12 11 10 09   6 5 4 3 2

Manufactured by Bang Printing, Brainerd, MN,
United States of America, September 2009

Light-Beams Publishing
10 Toon Lane, Lee, New Hampshire 03861

visit us at www.light-beams.com

The Fairy Houses Series® is a registered trademark of Light-Beams.Publishing

For my friend Judy Nerbonne, who planted the seeds and nurtured their growth

And for my husband Barry, whose talents brought in the harvest and created a feast!

- T. K.

For Kate and Meg ~ who fill my life with wonder and sweetness

For Mom and Dad ~ who gave me wings

- K. S.

We would like to thank our many friends and family members who read and reread different versions of this story, gave excellent suggestions, asked questions and provided much needed support! We couldn't have done it without you! Special heartfelt thanks go to Dana Rau, Dick Adams, and Pat and Judy Nerbonne ~ editors extraordinaire!

Area Map

Chapter ONE

Luke Carver looked up from pulling dandelions. The fog on the river was so heavy it was hard to tell where Prescott Park ended and the water began. He squinted, trying to make out shapes in the mist. It felt as if someone was watching him from behind the big maple tree. He was sure it wasn't Uncle Rick. His uncle was whistling by the fountain in the middle of the park.

Luke had lived near the ocean his whole life. He knew that hot summer weather and cold water made sea smoke. But the fog still spooked him. He shrugged and tugged another weed from the flower bed.

Then Luke took another look around. Prescott Park sat on the banks of the Piscataqua River, in Portsmouth, New Hampshire. On a clear day, he could stand at the edge of the river and see the state of Maine on the other side.

Luke picked up a trowel. He hated weeding. But he better not tell Uncle Rick that. Uncle Rick might give him one of his "Nature is Magic" speeches. He had already gotten an earful on the way to the park that morning. Luke rolled his eyes, remembering Uncle Rick's lecture about how dandelions had developed strong roots for survival. Let's see how tough you really are, thought Luke, as he yanked at a weed. He groaned as the plant snapped off, leaving the root in the ground.

A horn blasted in the distance. It was a boat signaling the bridge to raise its middle section. The fog was lifting. Luke spotted a tugboat chugging out toward the ocean. Gardening wasn't so bad. He could watch the action on the water. Plus, he could earn extra gas money for his boat. Maybe he would go fishing this afternoon with his friend Trevor. On second thought, maybe he should just go by himself.

Trevor was Luke's next door neighbor and his best buddy since kindergarten. But hanging out with Trevor hadn't been such a good idea lately.

Last week, Trevor almost talked Luke into taking his small boat six miles out to the Isles of Shoals. His parents would have—

"I think the dandelions are winning!" Luke jumped at the sound of his uncle's voice.

"Uncle Rick, I didn't see you coming," said Luke. "The sea smoke is—"

"Quiet," Uncle Rick said. "Don't move. He's right behind you."

"Who?" Luke turned to look in the direction of Uncle Rick's gaze. He saw a flash of brown dart into the trellis.

"It's that sneaky rabbit!" said Uncle Rick. "I've been trying to catch him for days. He's been devouring the flowers as fast as I plant them. See if you can herd him over to that maple tree where I've set a trap."

So that's who had been watching him! "You're not going to hurt him are you?" Luke asked. The rabbit peeked from behind the trellis and sniffed the air.

"Nah, it's a humane animal trap. I put some juicy carrots inside for bait. He'll hop in, the door will close behind him and he'll be just fine."

The rabbit headed toward a bed of petunias. Luke panicked. What if the rabbit ate all the flowers he had spent hours planting?

"We can't let that rabbit use Prescott Park gardens for his personal restaurant." Uncle Rick's hushed voice cut through his thoughts. "He's getting fatter than that tugboat over there."

Luke slowly approached the rabbit from behind. The rabbit leapt forward and dashed toward the maple. Instead of going into the trap, he veered to the left and disappeared down a hole between the tree's spreading roots.

"He got away," Luke said.

"Not again!" muttered Uncle Rick. "We'll have to wait 'til he gets hungry and pokes his nose out to smell those carrots." Rick picked up a pot of tulips. "When I finally capture him, I know a wooded area on the other side of the water where he can make a new home."

"You can't do that!" Luke replied. "There are

coyotes in the woods over there. Maybe I can take him home." Luke's house was nestled on the shore of Sagamore Creek, on the outskirts of Portsmouth, in a heavily wooded area full of deer, possum, raccoons, and great blue herons. "I could make him a hutch out of some of Dad's lobster pots." Then he added, "Mom wouldn't mind."

"Are you crazy? I've known your mother a lot longer than you have. She is my sister, you know!" laughed Uncle Rick. "She'd have a fit if I let you take that rabbit home for a pet. Besides, she's busy enough running her summer camp."

"But the campers are city kids from Boston. They come here to see the wildlife! They've probably never seen a live rabbit up close," Luke replied.

"Some wildlife," scoffed his uncle. "A chubby bunny that eats flowers and wiggles its nose." He shook his head and smiled. "No, it's definitely too scary for the city crowd. We wouldn't want the kids to have nightmares, would we?"

Luke chuckled at the idea. "I know," he said. "What if we just let him loose in my woods?"

"No way. I want him as far away from my flower beds as possible. Anyway, it's no use waiting for Peter Rabbit now." Uncle Rick bent over to pick up a shovel and trowel. "Let's pack up. We have to go over to Annie Lennox's place. She's hired me to look after her property this summer."

"Mrs. Lennox?" Luke said. "Uncle Rick, she hates me!"

"Then you'd better be on your best behavior," Uncle Rick replied. "Grab that rake behind you."

"Do I have to go?" Luke asked. He picked up the rake, which reminded him of the broom Mrs. Lennox was holding when she shooed him off her property last month. He was just taking a shortcut.

"Well, I thought you'd like to meet the new renters living in her cottage. The woman is really nice. She's the archeologist at Strawbery Banke Museum. She said she had a kid going into sixth grade. Won't that be your class?"

"A boy?" Luke asked, suddenly very interested in his uncle's plan.

"I forgot to ask," his uncle said, as he hopped into his truck. "Come on and we'll find out."

Luke jumped in beside his uncle. He had a new classmate to meet.

Chapter TWO

"This is a perfect place to build fairy houses," Kate Evans whispered in awe, as she came to a stand of tall pines. Her mom had said the cottage was near a wooded area, but this looked more like an enchanted forest. It was quiet, misty, and overflowing with green ferns and mosses. There was even a small stream that bubbled as it splashed over some rocks. Beams of sunlight filtered through the trees, creating warm spotlights between cool shadows. This was definitely better than she had imagined, and Kate had a vivid imagination.

She started collecting some fallen branches and pieces of bark. She was careful not to disturb the mosses and gently built around them by placing the sticks in a teepee shape on a bed of pine needles.

Kate had first learned about building fairy houses with her best friend, Laura. The girls had spent hours in a wooded area in Kate's old neighborhood, building fairy houses together. Kate thought Laura would love it here. If only she still lived right next door! Kate wondered if she would ever find a friend like Laura, someone who loved playing in the woods as she did.

"A *fairy goes a-wandering*," Kate sang as she gathered pinecones. She spied a mockingbird in a nearby bush. "Hello little bird, are you listening to me?" The bird warbled a few notes in reply and flew into the branches of a giant pine tree.

Kate looked high up into the tree's crown. Her eyes moved down the immense trunk to where it widened before disappearing into a carpet of soft needles. The spot looked inviting. She sat down and breathed in the pine scent around her. Then she leaned back into a furrow at the trunk's center.

"HEY!!!" Kate jumped. It felt like something had pushed on her back! She turned around. A piece of bark had swung open like a door. Astonished, she waited a few moments to see if anything might scurry out. When nothing did, she approached the hollow cautiously.

"I wonder if this is some animal's house."
She examined the door. It was made from a thin
piece of wood covered with tree bark. It had a

special latch that released when it was pushed. Kate peered into the dark opening, which was a bit larger than her head. Something inside caught the light.

"Is that a little table?" Kate wondered. She squinted harder into the tree's hollow. "Could those be chairs next to it? Animals don't use furniture."

Off in the distance, Kate heard her mother's voice. "KAAATE!"

"It's too dark inside. I'll need a flashlight," Kate said to herself. She carefully replaced the door over the secret opening and pushed gently. She felt a click; the door fit so snuggly it disappeared into the tree trunk.

Her mom called again, "KAAATE, where are you?"

"Coming!" Kate yelled. She raced toward home. "Mom's not going to believe this!"

When she reached the edge of the woods, Kate saw her mom talking to a man. A boy stood next to him. Her mom looked Kate's way and waved for her to join them.

"Kate, I'd like you to meet Rick Fernandez.

Mr. Fernandez works at Prescott Park near my office at Strawbery Banke. He's in charge of the gardens. And this is his nephew, Luke Carver. Luke just turned eleven like you."

Luke and Kate eyed each other warily. Both mumbled a quick "Hi." Kate noticed that Luke was a bit shorter than she was. He looked a lot like his uncle, with dark wavy hair and brown eyes.

"The gardens next door are beautiful," Kate's mom said. "Is that your work, too?"

"Your landlady, Annie Lennox, has cared for them for as long as I can remember," answered Uncle Rick. "But, her husband died a couple of years ago and since then she's lost interest in gardening. She just hired me to take over and manage the grounds, including this cottage you're renting."

"The house is enormous for only one person," said Mrs. Evans.

"Does she own the woods, too?" Kate asked.

"Yes, she does. Her property goes all the way back behind Sagamore Creek, the tidal creek that runs by Luke's house," his uncle replied.

"I know a few developers who would love to get their hands on thirty-five acres of land on the water!"

Luke found his voice, "My Dad and I go past her place in our boat all the time when I help him haul lobster traps. I've always thought the Lennox house looked haunted."

"That old house does look interesting," Uncle Rick laughed.

Kate glanced over the tops of the trees and saw the roof line of the house in the distance. She wondered what it would be like to live alone in such a huge place.

"Why don't you and Kate come to my sister's house tomorrow night for a lobster bake?" asked Luke's uncle.

Mrs. Evans' face lit up. "That sounds lovely," she said. She caught a glimpse of her daughter's doubtful expression, but continued, "We'll bring the dessert. Kate and I made a couple of blueberry pies this morning. Where do you live, Luke?"

"Oh, just down the road," said Luke, as he quickly hopped into his uncle's truck.

"He's usually not that shy," Uncle Rick chuckled. "It's down this road on the left, a gray house with the white porch. You can't miss it. Look for the lobster pots piled up near the garage."

"What time?" Kate's mom asked.

"How about six o'clock?" he replied, starting his truck. "That will give us a chance to clean up after work."

Kate and her mom watched the truck disappear down the dirt driveway. "Luke seems like a nice kid. Maybe he'll be your first friend in Portsmouth," her mother said.

Yeah, right, thought Kate. Just her luck that the nearest neighbor turned out to be a boy!

Chapter
THREE

The sun was just about to peek over the horizon as Luke quietly left his house and headed down to the dock. He had been thinking about that poor rabbit all night. He wanted to check on Uncle Rick's trap before anyone showed up at Prescott Park.

He walked the length of the dock and untied his skiff. He hopped aboard and pushed off, all in one swift motion. He fastened his life jacket, and then checked to see if the oars were stashed in place under the seat. Although he was only eleven, boating in and around the back channel of the Piscataqua River was second nature to him. Last year for his birthday, his parents had surprised him with this wooden skiff.

Luke started his motor and was off, skimming over the calm water of the inlet at the edge of his family's property. Friendly gulls circled overhead, squawking their morning

greetings. He'd reach Prescott Park in no time. He rounded the point and headed toward Clam Pit Island.

To his left, Luke could see Mrs. Lennox's property, which the local people called Creek Farm. From his vantage point on the water, the house seemed abandoned. It reminded him of a haunted house he had seen in a movie.

Mrs. Lennox seemed grouchy the few times Luke had met her. Uncle Rick said she had grown up here, playing and boating in the same area that Luke loved to explore. Luke couldn't picture Mrs. Lennox out here, speeding through the back channel and weaving around the little islands the way he did.

Luke spotted the Prescott Park dock and nosed the boat in that direction. In this main part of the mighty Piscataqua River, the tidal current could make steering difficult. He could feel the power of the water as it rushed out to the ocean. He pulled tight and gripped the handle of his motor.

All of a sudden, a speedboat came out of nowhere, straight for Luke's skiff. The driver saw

Luke at the last minute and veered to the right, going toward the back channel. The man waved his fist and shouted angrily at Luke, even though he was the one who almost ran Luke over. It was Trevor's dad.

"That was a close call," yelled the Harbormaster as Luke pulled up to the dock. "This part of the river is a no-wake zone and that guy's looking for an accident."

Luke stepped onto the dock. "Hi, Mr. Sewell. He sure surprised me. Mind if I tie 'er up for the day? I'm helping Uncle Rick with the gardens."

"Nope," answered the weathered seaman, smiling. "Say hello to your uncle. I'll see you this afternoon."

Luke knew he would have to hurry to beat Uncle Rick to the trap, because his uncle was an early riser. As he hustled along, he thought about how Trevor and Trevor's dad had both been acting strangely lately.

Just last week, Luke and Trevor had had a terrible fight. Trevor tried to convince Luke to jump off the steel bridge that connected Prescott Park with Peirce Island even though the sign posted on the bridge clearly said "No Jumping." The guys unloading their catches at the fishing wharf and a lady walking her dog would have seen them. Trevor had called Luke a wimp. But Luke didn't care. He just walked away. He didn't want to get in trouble just because his friend needed to break the rules to have fun.

Luke reached the spot where his uncle had left the trap. It was empty. Peter Rabbit was safe, at least for now.

Chapter FOUR

Since Luke's house was less than a mile away, Kate and her mom had decided to walk to the lobster bake. Kate hadn't had a moment to go exploring by herself since she had discovered the hidden room yesterday. All she could think about were the secrets that might lie in the hollowed-out tree trunk. She planned to bring a flashlight next time to see it better. Had she imagined the furniture or was it simply a squirrel house with some twigs inside?

"There's going to be a lovely sunset later," Mrs. Evans said.

Kate glanced at her mom's smiling face. Kate could tell that her mom liked it here. She knew her mother was excited about her new job, and maybe she even liked Mr. Fernandez a little, too. He looked different from her Dad, who had died when Kate was too young to remember. Still, she knew his face from the family photos. In fact, everyone always said that Kate looked just like him, especially her blue eyes with tiny flecks of gold and her thick, chestnut-colored hair. Anyway, she would have to keep an eye on Mr. Fernandez and make sure he was good enough for her mom.

"This must be the place," Kate's mom said. "See the lobster traps? And that's Rick's truck in the driveway."

A woman stepped out onto the porch. "Greetings," she said. "You must be Rick's guests." She was pretty, with her curly brown hair pulled back in a ponytail. "I'm Connie Carver, Rick's twin sister," she said.

"Thanks for inviting us for dinner," said Kate's mom. "Here are some pies we baked."

A small figure stepped out from behind Mrs. Carver. "Oh. And this is my daughter, Meg."

"And I'm four," declared the little girl with two long braids.

"Hi, Meg," said Kate. "I like your hair."

"Dinner will be ready shortly," Mrs. Carver said. "Come meet my husband."

Passing through the kitchen, they came out into a long narrow backyard that ended at the water. At the far edge sat a shed and a dock with two boats tied to it, a lobster boat and a smaller skiff.

"This is my husband, Kevin," Mrs. Carver said. Luke's dad stood alongside Uncle Rick, helping with the lobster bake. They had built a fire in a hole in the ground with rocks lining the bottom. The seaweed they had piled over it hissed and steamed.

Just then, a large boy in a Red Sox cap came charging into the yard shouting, "Luke, come on. We'll miss the lobsters getting thrown into the fire!" He turned to look back at Luke, who seemed to be stalling at the backyard gate. Luke followed slowly behind.

"Luke doesn't like this part of the cookout," his father explained. "That's why he usually shows up after the food is ready. This, by the way, is our next door neighbor, Trevor. He's joining us for dinner tonight. We can't keep him away when we're cooking lobster. Trevor, this is Mrs. Evans and her daughter, Kate."

Trevor looked at Kate suspiciously. "Ever seen a lobster before?"

"Sure," Kate said. "We moved here from

Maine and—"

"Don't ya' just love watching them get thrown in the fire?" Trevor interrupted. "They change color as they get cooked alive. Sometimes you can hear them scream! They look like giant red insects!"

"Lobsters are crustaceans," Kate said coolly. "They don't actually feel pain, but you can sometimes hear the whistling sound of steam escaping from their wet shells."

"Duh! I knew that," Trevor replied. "I'm always telling people that Luke's dad catches crustigans."

"Kate?" a small voice asked. "Do you want to come see the hop-toad houses?"

"Hop-toad houses?" said Kate. Meg took her hand and led her toward the pottery shed.

"Yeah, I want to see the itty-bitty toad homes, don't you, Luke?" Trevor taunted and followed without waiting for Luke's reply.

"This is where Mom makes her clay pots," Meg explained. "But sometimes when she bakes them, they crack. Then she puts them in the garden for the hop-toads to live in."

"A lot of toads have moved into them," Luke said.

Kate bent down to get a closer look at one of the upside-down pots. It had an opening where it had cracked. "I think I see a pair of eyes peeking out at me," she said softly.

"That's Hoppy," Meg announced. "He's my favorite!"

"Lemme see!" Trevor pushed Kate aside. He grabbed the clay pot and lifted it high in the air to expose a startled toad. "Whoa," he said, "This looks like a tasty little treat for my pet snake, Slither."

"Nooooo!" Meg screamed, her eyes growing wide with terror.

Before Trevor could seize the small toad, Luke grabbed his arm. "Stop it, Trevor," Luke said. "That's Meg's pet."

"Oh, yeah," Trevor snorted. "Some pet."

Kate looked at Meg's stricken face. Her eyes flashed at Trevor. "Isn't it funny how bullies always seem to pick on someone half their size!"

Trevor sneered. "Great! Another nature freak!"

"Trevor!" Luke stepped between Kate and his friend. "Cut it out."

But before he could continue there was a shout from the house.

"Dinner's ready," Luke's dad called. "Come and get it!"

Chapter FIVE

The kids' hot tempers soon cooled when their appetites took over. They sat at the large picnic table on the deck. It was covered with newspapers. Luke's mom passed out bibs for everyone to wear because lobster bakes were definitely messy!

Uncle Rick was helping Meg crack open her lobster when Trevor reached across for his third helping of corn.

"I think you've had enough there, buddy," Uncle Rick said.

"Yes, save some room for Kate's blueberry pie," Luke's mom added.

Trevor glared at Kate from across the table.

Kate ignored him and turned to Luke's dad. "Mr. Carver," she asked, "could I please have the empty mussel shells and some of the corn husks to take home?"

Everyone stopped eating and looked up.

"Sure thing," Mr. Carver said. "What do you want them for?"

Kate flushed. "Oh, I need some natural materials, ah . . . to decorate some bird houses. It's a summer project."

She stole a look at her mom who gave her a secret smile. Her mom knew Kate really wanted them to build fairy houses.

"Why would birds want houses made from garbage?" Trevor asked.

"Sounds pretty resourceful to me," Uncle Rick said.

Mrs. Carver laughed. "I remember when Luke found out that baby birds were born without feathers. He used to brush our cat and leave the loose fur on the deck. He watched the birds take it and said they were using it for blankets."

"Gimme a break!" mocked Trevor.

"I was only five years old," Luke said defensively.

Laughter rose softly around the table. "Do you think I should use some cat fur in the hop-toad houses?" Meg piped in.

Everyone laughed louder.

"Mom," Luke said, changing the subject, "are

there any marshmallows left?"

"Sure. I think they're in the cupboard over the refrigerator. I'll check."

"I saved the sticks we used last time," Luke said. "They're out behind the kiln."

"I'll get them!" Trevor jumped up from the table. He headed toward the pottery shed. After a few moments, he returned with the sticks in one hand and his baseball cap in the other.

"I think I'm gonna' go," Trevor said.

"Heading home before dessert?" Uncle Rick said, raising his eyebrows. "Wait a minute." He stopped clearing the table. "What's that moving in your cap, Trevor?"

The little brown head of a toad poked over the brim as it struggled to crawl out.

"Hoppy!" Meg cried. Luke reached out just in time to catch the toad as it jumped.

"Trevor," Luke said. "I don't get you." Then, he turned to his sister. "Don't worry, Meg. We'll put Hoppy back into his house right now." Meg followed Luke toward the shed, as he carefully cupped both hands around the toad.

"Gotta' go," Trevor mumbled. He left

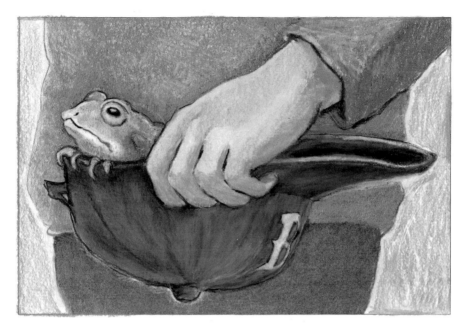

through the side gate before anyone could ask
him what he had planned to do with Hoppy.

Once Trevor was gone, Mr. and Mrs. Carver
set the pies on the table. Uncle Rick helped the
children toast the marshmallows at the fire pit.
After dessert, Uncle Rick offered to give Mrs.
Evans and Kate a ride home.

Kate's mom glanced up at the sky. It had
turned a vivid shade of violet blue, and the
first stars were twinkling in the distance. The
moon sat near the horizon, a gigantic yellow orb

casting strobes of light over the water. "It's such a beautiful night. I think we'll walk."

Kate and her mom said their goodbyes and began strolling toward home. Kate held the bag of mussel shells and corn husks. Should she tell her Mom about the secret house? Maybe she should wait. One thing was for sure though; she would never, ever, tell Trevor and hoped he never ventured into the woods. He was probably too busy playing video games or watching TV. Luke, on the other hand, seemed more like an outdoor type. He obviously liked animals. But share her secrets with him? Not if he's hanging out with someone like Trevor!

Chapter SIX

The next morning Kate joined her mom at Strawbery Banke Museum. Mrs. Evans gave her a tour of the historic homes, all restored to different periods of time. Kate tried to imagine being a sea captain's daughter two hundred years ago, or living on food rations during World War II. But her mind kept drifting to the discovery she had made in the woods. She wanted to go back to get a closer look.

"What's up?" Mrs. Evans asked, as they walked across the museum's big lawn. "You've been awfully quiet this morning."

"Nothing much," Kate responded.

"Are you sure you're okay?"

"Mom, I'm fine," Kate replied. "I was just thinking about this spot I discovered in the woods behind the cottage. It's perfect for building fairy houses."

"Is that where you're going this afternoon?" her mom asked. "In that case, you need a hearty meal." They headed to the museum's restaurant.

As soon as lunch was over, Kate raced home on her bicycle. She stepped inside the cottage to grab a flashlight, the mussel shells and corn husks from the lobster bake. The woods started at the edge of the lawn. In the distance, Kate could see Mrs. Lennox's house. She entered the woods and quietly made her way along the path until she saw the fairy house she had built. She scouted out the tree with the secret door. She had to push on the trunk in several places before she found the right spot.

"Anybody in there?" Kate spoke softly as she took the flashlight from her pocket and clicked it on.

She pointed the beam of light inside the hollow and gasped. It was a small room! Kate could make out something that looked like a table made from stone. It was surrounded by four little seashell chairs. Kate moved in to get a closer look. She could even see tiny scallop shells that looked like bowls on the table. Everything had a layer of dust on it, as if it had been there a long time.

"What are you doing?" said a voice behind her.

Startled, Kate bumped her head on the trunk above the opening. She jumped up and came face to face with Luke. "Uhmm, nothing," she said, trying to stay calm.

"Right," Luke replied. "I didn't mean to surprise you. It's just that Uncle Rick and I were working in Mrs. Lennox's gardens and we saw you head into the woods. We thought you might be collecting stuff for the birdhouses you talked about last night. Anyway, we found this starfish and I . . . I mean we . . . thought you might want to use it."

Kate gave him a doubtful look.

Luke held out the starfish like a peace offering.

"Thank you," said Kate as she took it.

Luke looked around. "Is that your birdhouse?" He had noticed Kate's fairy house on the ground. "Because if it is, I hope you know that birds won't use it. Birds need to make their nests in trees to keep their eggs safe."

"I know that," Kate said. "It's . . . ahh,

I mean . . . I made it for . . . umm." Kate noticed an orange and black butterfly fly into the secret opening she had discovered in the tree trunk. "Butterflies! I made this house for the butterflies to use . . . for shelter, you know, if it rains or something."

Luke looked at Kate skeptically and then bent down for a closer look. He smiled. "Good idea. I like it. It reminds me of Mom's toad houses, only more natural."

"You think?" Kate smiled.

"Did you make one inside this tree, too?" Luke headed toward the open door of the trunk. He kneeled down and peeked inside. "It's hard to see inside. Can I use your flashlight?"

Kate wasn't sure she wanted him to see her discovery. "Wow!" he said. "You built a table? And . . . are those chairs?"

Kate found herself handing him the flashlight. "Actually, I didn't build this furniture."

"And I think I even see a bed!" Luke said. "Wait a minute...what are these things?" He reached into the cavity and pulled out a small

scallop shell with two halves closed tightly together like a miniature treasure chest. He handed it to Kate.

"I don't know," she said. "I didn't make this house. It was already here in the tree. I sort of discovered it. Look at this door. It had to be made by someone who knows a lot about building."

Luke closed the door and pushed gently to release it again. "Whoa!"

"How many shell boxes are there?" asked Kate.

"I'm not sure," Luke reached in and pulled out a couple more. "If you didn't make it . . . then who did?"

"I don't know," Kate sighed as she shook one of the shells. "Hey, something's rattling inside. I wonder what it could be."

Kate gently pressed her finger against the place where the two halves met. The shell sprang open and something fell to the ground.

"Is that a tooth!?" Luke picked up the small pearly object.

"I think so." Kate looked at it from over

Luke's shoulder. "And it's not an animal's," she said with mounting excitement. "I think it's . . . a kid's tooth!"

Kate hurried to open the other shell boxes as Luke handed them out to her. There were seven altogether and each one contained a small tooth!

Kate took the flashlight and guided the beam of light around the interior of the tree. She could see all the furniture clearly. Near the table and chairs sat a bed made from a large clamshell, with feathers in it. After a long moment she whispered, "I can't believe this! I think we've discovered a Tooth Fairy's house!"

"**Tooth Fairy!**" Luke exclaimed.

Just then, the butterfly Kate had seen earlier flew out of the tree trunk where it had been hiding. For a moment, Luke thought he'd just seen a fairy come out. He glanced back down at the seven little teeth. "I think I need another look."

Kate handed the flashlight to Luke. His head seemed to disappear into the massive tree. Then he backed out and reached into the opening and took out a flat stone.

"Look!" he said. "This was behind the bed. It has some writing on it!"

The stone was a bit dusty, but Luke could make out the words.

"*If you discover this tooth fairy's house,*
There is another yet to find.
Built big enough for a mole or a mouse,
By fairies of a different kind."

"Hey. Do you think there might be more around here?" Luke thumped his fist against another tree trunk. "Ouch! Well, not this one. . . ."

"A mystery!" said Kate.

"We'll have to wait to solve it," Luke said. "I have to get back to help Uncle Rick."

"Oh," said Kate.

"How about we meet here tomorrow at the same time and try to solve the secret of the hidden fairy house, like who built it and when and whether there was a crime involved?" Luke smiled mischievously. "I always thought I'd make a good detective."

"Yeah, sure," Kate giggled. "While you're weeding, why don't you try to figure out what 'fairies of a different kind' means, Mr. Sherlock Holmes!"

"Who?" Luke asked.

"Sherlock Holmes," she answered. "He was a famous detective from England who solved mysteries with his friend, Dr. Watson."

"See you tomorrow, Watson!" he called as he walked toward the Lennox home.

Chapter SEVEN

Kate arrived at the pine tree the next day to find Luke bent over the small stream that meandered through the woods. She watched him place something in the water.

"Hello," Kate said.

Luke looked up. "Hey. I didn't hear you coming."

"What are you doing?" asked Kate.

"I'm making a raft," he said. Luke tied some twigs together with slender reeds. "I used to make these all the time when I was younger, for the gnomes to sail on."

"Gnomes?" Kate said. The raft reminded Kate of the furniture she made for fairies. "You know, I've often thought that gnomes must be friends of the fairies."

"You think they hang out together?" Luke asked.

"Are you teasing me?" answered Kate.

"Not really," Luke smiled.

"Even though you can't see them, I still think

they're all around us, just invisible to our eyes," Kate said, "kind of like sound waves. I think my cat can see them, especially at night. I think other animals might see them, too."

"Interesting," Luke pondered. "I guess smells are like that."

"Smells?" Kate asked.

"Sure, you know . . . odors. You can smell them, right? And they definitely exist; some smell good and some smell bad . . . disgusting even, but we can't see them. They're invisible, just like the gnomes and fairies."

Kate's face lit up with a smile.

"Uncle Rick always says nature's magic is all around us," Luke continued. "Look at the tadpoles swimming around my gnome boat. Pretty soon they'll be frogs. See how some of them already have their back legs?" He pointed to a cluster of them in a quiet area of the water.

"Like a caterpillar turning into a butterfly," Kate said.

"Right!" Luke scooped up a loose lily pad floating by and attached it to a small stick that had fallen from a tree. Then he stuck it into the top of his raft, creating a sail. He launched the miniature boat and watched it drift down the stream.

"Look at that!" Luke suddenly pointed to a tree limb just above where the boat was heading. "It's a nymph!"

"A nymph? Is that like a fairy?" Kate asked. "Where?"

"On that branch, right there! A nymph, a dragonfly larva," Luke said. "Don't you know where dragonflies come from?"

"Eggs?" Kate asked.

"Yeah, eggs first, which then hatch into larvae, called nymphs," Luke said. "Nymphs look like beetles. They live in the water. You'd never believe it, but a dragonfly will break out of there, dry its wings like a butterfly and take off." Luke hopped over to a rock. "And look here!" He pointed to a dry casing. "This is the hard skin of another nymph. There's the small hole on its back where the dragonfly came out."

Kate stared at the empty shell with its six legs. It looked like the skeleton of a prehistoric bug. She couldn't imagine a delicate dragonfly coming from that suit of bulky armor. As if reading her thoughts, a large dragonfly hovered in front of her face like a helicopter, its green eyes glittering in the sun.

Luke and Kate watched, riveted, as it flitted off, over to a stone wall covered by moss. It landed there for a moment.

"It's almost like he wants us to follow him over there," whispered Kate.

"Fairies of a different kind," said Luke, remembering the line in the clue. "I wonder . . ." He looked at the gnarly roots of a maple tree sticking up between the rocks of the stone wall. "Those smaller pebbles don't look like they're part of the wall."

As they approached the wall, the dragonfly disappeared into a small hole among the moss-covered roots. Kate bent down to peer into the opening. "Luke! I think I see a room."

"Look! These pointy shapes look like roof tops," said Luke. "They're just hidden under the moss. Let's take off the small stones and see what's behind them."

They worked together, carefully moving one

stone at a time. Kate's heart was pounding. She thought she could see some small furniture. Luke removed more pebbles. "Wow," he exclaimed.

"Let me see," Kate said. Inside was a room nestled among the tree roots. It was a kitchen with a table and two benches. There was a fireplace and a pantry with a tiny broom in the corner. Acorn cap bowls lined the shelves.

Luke found another pile of pebbles about a foot away. He called out to Kate.

"There's a bed in here!" Luke said.

"And a tiny green skirt and a red pointed hat and . . . are those shoes?" Kate said.

"Gnomes wear red pointed hats," said Luke. "And leather boots like those. I read once that they like to build their homes underground around tree roots."

Luke smiled. "Watson, I do believe we've solved the mystery. What we have here is a gnome house and—"

"Luke!" Kate interrupted. "There's another stone. It was behind the bed again!" She reached in and pulled it out gently. She could barely make out the words, so she blew on it. Flecks of dirt and dust scattered into the air.

"Hurry up and read it, will you?" Luke said.

"Okay, okay." Kate began to read:

"This is a gnome home you've discovered,
It leads to another, hidden from sight.
In secret splendor and lying covered,
Revealed to you by the full moon's light."

"Another one?" Luke gasped. "This is unbelievable! I've never heard of anyone finding gnome homes and tooth fairy houses."

"And that's why we should keep it a secret," Kate said.

Luke looked at Kate. "I won't tell anyone," he said.

"Not Trevor?" Kate asked.

"Especially not Trevor," Luke said. "Look, the moon will be bright tonight and it'll rise around five o'clock."

"How do you know that?" asked Kate.

"Because I noticed the moon at the lobster bake. As it gets bigger, the moon rises about one hour later each day."

"You're a real nature geek, you know that?" Kate smiled.

"It takes one to know one." Luke said. "So, can we meet here later tonight? Maybe the moon will reveal something."

"After dinner," Kate agreed. "Let's meet at eight o'clock by the tooth fairy tree. It'll be getting dark by then."

"It's a date! I mean . . . I'll see you later, Watson." Luke added. He turned and headed toward home.

Chapter
EIGHT

"That was some thunderstorm we had last night," Uncle Rick said. He and Luke were driving to Mrs. Lennox's house early the next morning to check on her gardens before going to Prescott Park.

"Yeah, Mom made me stay home." Luke frowned. He hadn't been able to meet Kate. He wondered when they would have a chance to go to back to the woods to find the next clue.

"Good. That means that you're rested and ready to do some hard labor today. We have a lot of mulch to spread."

"We have to check on the trap as soon as we get there," said Luke. "You haven't caught Peter Rabbit yet, have you?"

"Not yet. I saw him helping himself to the petunias yesterday." His uncle frowned.

"When we do catch him, can we let him go in the woods here?" asked Luke.

"I don't think so. Mrs. Lennox doesn't want to feed him either," said Uncle Rick.

"He doesn't eat that much! What about near our house, then?" Luke said. He had to find a way to convince Uncle Rick to release the rabbit somewhere safe.

"We'll see. First we have to weed Mrs. Lennox's garden. I hope the flowers didn't get damaged by the hard rain. I guess we'll see soon enough." Uncle Rick pulled up to the courtyard by the house.

They unloaded the wheelbarrow, shovels, and trowels from the back of the truck. Luke looked up and noticed the tower on the house had a clock face on it. One of the hands was bent, like a gnarly finger gesturing to him.

Uncle Rick interrupted his thoughts. "Go knock on Mrs. Lennox's door and let her know that we're here. I'll meet you in the garden."

Luke started to protest, but his uncle was already halfway across the lawn. He thought back to his last encounter with Mrs. Lennox, when she had yelled at him for walking across her property. He kicked at the dirt. Then he took a granola bar from his shirt pocket and peeled the wrapper off as he walked slowly

toward the house.

"If you think you are going to get crumbs on my front porch, think again, young man," snapped a voice from inside the screen door. Mrs. Lennox stood with her hands on her hips, a stern expression on her face.

"Um . . . Good morning, Mrs. Lennox," stammered Luke as he stopped at the bottom of the steps. "My uncle and I are here to work in your garden."

"Make sure you take care of that wrapper. I don't want any litter on my front lawn."

Luke looked down at the granola bar in his hand. He glanced back at the door and Mrs. Lennox was gone. He quickly made his way to the garden before she had a chance to come out and yell at him again.

"Hey, Uncle Rick," called Luke.

"Over here. Look at this!" His uncle pointed to the white fence that ran from the edge of the garage to the garden. It was covered with bright blue, yellow, and red spray paint. There were angry swirls and marks and words that Luke couldn't make out.

"Who would do this?" said Uncle Rick.

"I don't know," Luke said.

"And look at the gardens!" Uncle Rick stared at the flower beds, torn up, flowers ripped from the ground. "That was not caused by last night's storm."

"Definitely not a rabbit either," said Luke.

"I just can't imagine who would do this to such a nice lady," Uncle Rick said. "How about if you straighten up the garden while I go talk to Mrs. Lennox."

"Good idea," agreed Luke. He knelt down and gently placed an uprooted plant into the ground. He continued down the row, one plant at a time. Suddenly, he caught a glimpse of something out of the corner of his eye.
A hummingbird was still able to feed from one of the upturned daylilies.

Chapter NINE

"Did you bring your flashlight?" Kate asked Luke as they headed into the woods at dusk. It was a clear night and the moon was already visible in the sky overhead.

"Yeah. And some brownies my mom baked today."

"Brownies?" Kate laughed.

"We're going to need some energy to help us figure out this clue," Luke said.

"I brought water," Kate said. "Some for us and some to leave in this large clamshell for the fairies and gnomes, in case they get thirsty."

"That shell's big enough for a gnome bathtub," said Luke, "or maybe even a fairy swimming pool."

Luke halted. Kate peered over his shoulder. She could see Trevor in the beam of Luke's flashlight, crouching beside her fairy house. He was shoving his pudgy fingers in and knocking over some of the leaning twigs.

Trevor looked up at them. "Soooo. **This**

56

is where you've been spending all your time, Luke," Trevor sneered. Kate felt herself go cold, her eyes narrowing as Trevor continued. "Building **fairy houses**? I can't believe it! And with a **girl**?"

"Trevor, what are you doing here?" Luke asked in a calm voice.

"I followed you here the other day," Trevor answered. "I could hear you talking about fairies and gnome homes. When did you turn into such a wimp?"

He kicked at Kate's fairy house. "This is nothing but a bunch of sticks, like a campfire just waiting to be lit. So I came to help you out."

Trevor pulled a lighter from his pocket and flicked it open. He placed the flame near the top of the fairy house and the dry leaves on the little roof ignited instantly. A furry mouse darted out.

Kate sprang into action, her body fueled with fury. She ran toward her fairy house and unscrewed the top of her water bottle.

Trevor stared down, smiling at his handiwork. A burning leaf drifted up with the

smoke and headed toward his mop of curly hair. Within seconds Trevor's hair started smoking.

"Stay still, Trevor!" Kate shouted. She turned her aim to Trevor and squeezed her water bottle. The water sprayed the top of Trevor's head and trickled down onto his face.

"Hey!!" Trevor sputtered. A trace of smoke rose from his hair. Luke grabbed a hunk of wet mossy ground. He rubbed it on top of Trevor's head.

At the same time, Kate went to work on the fairy house. She doused it with water and the flames went out.

"What are you doing!!?" Trevor screamed. "Get away from me." He shoved Luke away. Then he stumbled toward the path without looking back. "You guys are going to regret this!"

"You'd think he'd be a little more grateful," Kate said.

Luke frowned. "I don't think he even realized his hair was on fire."

Kate and Luke covered the fairy house with dirt to make sure the fire was completely out. Now, it looked like a teepee made from mud.

"It's cool to the touch," Luke said when the teepee stopped sending out smoke signals. "But your house is ruined!"

"I can fix it," she said. "But Trevor could have set these whole woods on fire! What's wrong with him?"

"I really don't know," Luke said. "He's been doing some strange things lately, but not this bad. This is Mrs. Lennox's land. She wouldn't let us come here if she knew what happened."

"That's why we need to keep it a secret," Kate reminded him. She peered up at the night sky. "It's too cloudy for the moonlight to reveal anything now," Kate sighed. "I guess we should just go home."

They headed out of the woods. They would try again the next moonlit night.

Chapter TEN

The following morning Kate stopped by her mom's office at Strawbery Banke. Mrs. Evans sat at her desk, paging through a book. An old photograph lay on top of a pile of papers next to her. Kate picked it up and studied the photo showing three children playing in the woods.

"Isn't that a great picture?" Mrs. Evans asked.

"These kids are dressed in costumes," Kate said.

"They're Mrs. Lennox's relatives," Mrs. Evans said. "They used to live in the Whitcomb Mansion down the road from Mrs. Lennox's house. The photo was taken almost a hundred years ago. I'm reading a book that was written by Mrs. Lennox's mom." Mrs. Evans tapped the book in her hand. "It's about the wonderful adventures they had growing up around Sagamore Creek. They sometimes dressed up as fairies."

Dressed as fairies, Kate thought. "Mom, could I make a copy of the picture?"

"Sure," her mom said. She ran the photo through the copy machine in the office.

"You know, Kate," said Mrs. Evans, "these children remind me of you. Do you think they built fairy houses, too?"

Kate stared at the picture. One girl seemed to be looking directly at her. She hadn't had a chance to tell her mom about the mystery houses she and Luke had discovered. Maybe this was the time to tell her.

"Mom," she started, "You know the woods behind Mrs. Lennox's house where I go sometimes—"

Kate was interrupted by a swift knock at the door. Luke's uncle poked his head in. "Can I interest anyone here in joining me for a bowl of chowder down at Geno's?" Uncle Rick asked. "My treat," he added with a charming smile.

"You sure do know the way to these two girls' hearts," Kate's mom laughed. "How'd you know that clam chowder is a family favorite?"

"Intuition," he replied. "Truthfully, I have some other news for you."

"Let's go then," said Kate. They headed down

the street toward the neighborhood chowder house.

"Someone vandalized Annie's property. We discovered it yesterday," Luke's uncle said as they turned onto Mechanic Street. "They sprayed graffiti on her fence and tore up the flower beds. Have either of you seen anything suspicious lately?"

"That's terrible!" said Kate's mom. "I haven't seen anyone, have you, Kate?"

"Hmm . . . in the garden?" Kate stalled remembering Trevor's near fire in the woods. "Nope, no one in the garden." Why hadn't Luke told her about it yesterday?

At Geno's, they sat at a table on the deck overlooking the water and Peirce Island. Uncle Rick pointed to a spot on the other side of the river, right at the edge. "Look! A Great Blue Heron. A few years ago, it was rare to see one around here. Now that we're making an effort to keep our water clean, we see them all the time. They come for the seafood, just like us!"

The waitress took their orders for chowder. After she left, Uncle Rick continued. "There's something else that concerns Annie Lennox. There's a meeting at seven tonight. A developer has made an offer to buy her property. We want to know what they're planning to put there. It could change the whole town. And it certainly would affect you and Kate, since your house is part of her property."

"That doesn't sound good at all," said Kate's mom. The waitress placed three steaming bowls of chowder in front of them. "I think we need to go to that meeting, don't you, Kate?"

Kate thought about the enchanted forest and the secret fairy houses. What would become of them? Was Mrs. Lennox selfish enough to sell her property to developers? "Mom, we definitely need to go!" Kate answered.

Chapter ELEVEN

"What would happen to the wildlife?" asked Luke.

Luke's parents had invited Kate and her mom over, along with Uncle Rick, to discuss the outcome of the meeting. The dining room table was littered with coffee mugs and brownie crumbs. Luke's question hung in the air. They could hear a chorus of crickets drift in from the window, as if to ask, how will you save us?

"Do you think Mrs. Lennox would actually sell her land?" Kate asked.

"Oh, no! Hop-toads live there," said Luke's sister Meg.

"Well," said Uncle Rick, "her property is one of the most valuable pieces of land along the seacoast. It's getting harder for her to care for it as she gets older."

"The developers can't just dig up the shoreline of the creek next to Annie's house to build a big hotel and marina," Mrs. Carver said.

Mr. Carver's brow furrowed. "There are laws in place to protect wetlands."

"It would be a shame to knock down such a unique home," Kate's mom said. "The property borders Annie's childhood home, the historic Whitcomb Mansion. I've been reading a book by Annie's mother about the adventures she had with her brothers and sisters. It makes a fascinating story."

"The kids in the picture?" asked Kate.

Her mom nodded.

Mrs. Carver peered into her coffee as if searching for something. "If only Annie could be convinced to donate the land to the city or the state. Then it could be protected. That's what her parents did with the Whitcomb property."

Kate realized there was a lot more at stake than just saving the fairy houses. She couldn't help wondering if the houses were a key to a solution. She looked at Luke. Could she and Luke convince Mrs. Lennox not to sell her land?

"By the way, Rick, have you found out who vandalized Mrs. Lennox's gardens?" asked Mrs. Evans.

"No, not a clue," he answered. "But Annie is really spooked by it."

"Do you think it could be Trevor?" asked Mrs. Carver.

"What makes you think that, Mom?" Luke said.

"His parents are having a hard time. They're getting a divorce and Trevor and his mom are moving to Maryland in a few weeks. He's really struggling with the news," his mom replied.

Kate caught Luke's eye and he nodded. They both got up and started heading to the deck.

"Where are you two going?" asked Mrs. Carver.

"Can we be excused? We're getting a little tired of all this grown-up talk."

The adults laughed. "Go ahead," answered Luke's dad.

"Can I go, too?" asked Meg.

"Bedtime for you, Kiddo." Mr. Carver pushed back from the table. "I'll tuck you in."

Kate followed Luke out onto the back porch. "Did you know about Trevor's parents?" whispered Kate.

"No, but it makes sense," answered Luke.

"You didn't tell me about Mrs. Lennox's garden!" Kate said. "Do you think Trevor did it? He was there, because he followed us."

"I don't know. Do you think we should tell our parents?"

"Not yet," said Kate. "If we do that, they might not let us go back into the woods. Then we wouldn't be able to find the next clue and solve the mystery! I have an idea. Do you have a camera?"

"Yeah. In fact I won a blue ribbon at school for

a photo I took of the Whaleback Lighthouse. I should show it to you." Luke smiled.

"Great," Kate said. "Can you take some pictures of the fairy houses?" Before she had time to explain, Mrs. Evans called her.

"I'll take the pictures tomorrow morning," Luke said as Kate turned to go. "Then we'll meet in the woods after dinner."

Chapter
TWELVE

Kate dashed out of the house at dusk. She
and her mom had eaten dinner, so Kate had
some time to repair her fairy house before Luke
met her in the woods. She carried a bag with
supplies to fix the house, and a large envelope to
fix something else. She hoped Luke had already
taken the photos. She couldn't wait to tell him
her plan.

When she arrived at the pine tree, Kate
placed the envelope on a large flat rock.
Kneeling at her house, Kate surveyed Trevor's
damage. She started clearing away the mud and
picking off the pieces that had been charred
by the flames. Kate reached into her bag and
brought out a few seashells. She thought these
would cheer things up. As she placed the shells
at the base of the structure, a pinecone fell from
the tree and bounced off her shoulder. Kate
ignored it. But another one crashed down on
top of the fairy house. A third one hit her back.

"Ouch!" Kate looked up into the pine tree.

Trevor sat on a sturdy branch, his cap casting a shadow over his eyes. He was poised to hurl another pinecone.

"What's your problem?" Kate yelled. A fourth cone struck another blow to the fairy house. "You ruined it once already."

"It's called **revenge**!" Trevor hunted around the branches looking for more pinecones. "For the mud bath you gave me yesterday. My mom blamed me for coming home filthy."

"But your hair was smoking! It was practically on fire!" Kate exclaimed.

Trevor threw another pinecone. "My dad was furious."

"Look," Kate began, "I know you have problems."

"You don't know anything about me," he said.

"I heard your folks are splitting up and you and your mom are moving to Maryland. But you'll still be able to come back and visit your dad," Kate encouraged, "and see your old friends. You can make new friends, too."

"Friends! What do you know about friends?"

Trevor snapped. "All you do is build stupid houses because you don't have any friends. Who told you about my parents, anyway?"

"What difference does it make?" Kate said. "I know how you feel."

"Are you an expert on divorce now, too?" Trevor said.

Kate clenched her fists. "No, not divorce. At least with divorce you still have a father. My father died right after I was born. I can't see him, not ever, never! You still have a dad. You still get to share the good times."

Trevor stared down at Kate, her face red, her eyes slit in anger.

"Yeah, right, the good times." Trevor sneered as he plucked a pinecone off a branch and pitched it at the teepee. He searched around the branches for more. "You have no idea, Miss Queen-of-the-Fairies, not a clue. By the way, where are your little friends with wings now that you need their help?" He found a pinecone and gave it a fierce tug.

Kate heard buzzing. Suddenly Trevor was surrounded by a black cloud. He had disturbed a beehive in the tree.

Trevor cursed and flailed his arms and legs, like a giant whirligig in a windstorm. He lost his balance and tumbled down, bouncing from branch to branch. He landed on his butt with a thud. Howling, he jumped to his feet and took off in a flash, tearing through the brush with the swarm chasing behind.

Kate was amazed. The angry bees hadn't seemed to notice her at all. It was as if they knew she meant them no harm. Still, she shouldn't stay there waiting for the swarm to return. The bees needed to calm down first. Really, she needed to calm down. She walked along the path. Even though the moon was bright, the thick canopy of leaves created dark tunnels.

Kate had been stung, but not by bees. Trevor's angry words had stung her. Was it true that fairies were her only friends?

"Kate," Luke yelled, the shaft of light from his flashlight bobbing up and down as he approached.

"I'm over here," Kate said with a smile.

Chapter THIRTEEN

"I brought the photos you wanted." Luke handed them to her. "I took them this morning after Uncle Rick and I cleaned up the mess in Mrs. Lennox's yard. My favorite one is the gnome home. The sun was shining on it just right when I took it."

"These are great!" Kate flipped through the pictures under Luke's flashlight. "I like the way the shells in the tooth fairy's house sparkle in this one."

"Wow, there are a lot of fireflies out tonight," Luke noticed as he sat next to Kate. "Maybe the moonlight attracts them."

"I think they're admiring your photos," Kate laughed. Two fireflies landed on the gnome house picture. They were joined by some others. Within minutes, Kate and Luke were surrounded by little flashing lights.

"I've never seen them so friendly," Luke said. "They tickle."

Kate giggled. "Luke, you look like a

Christmas tree covered in blinking gold lights."

The fireflies rose above them in a magical twinkling cloud, and then flew off toward a stand of trees.

"It would be easy to believe they're fairies," Kate said, as the small flickering dots landed on a tall mossy tree stump.

The moon emerged from behind a cloud. A shaft of moonlight pierced the tree's canopy, illuminating the stump. Kate and Luke approached the tree's remains. Dancing in the spotlight, the fireflies were almost invisible. They slowly scattered and headed off into the woods.

"Awesome! Look at that!" Luke said. "Doesn't it look like a roof with a chimney sticking up? Or a turret from a castle? I bet that's our fairy house hidden from sight!"

"Come on, Sherlock. We need to investigate." Kate knelt down at the stump. She brushed off some leaves and dislodged a large chunk of wood. "This isn't attached to the trunk! It's a piece of driftwood!"

She moved the wood, exposing a miniature stone wall with a door and a window. "Luke! It even has a door knob!"

Luke carefully removed the other pieces of driftwood and uncovered a stone turret with a peaked roof made of mussel shells. "Doesn't it seem like the house was built inside the stump? I think it's older than the other two. It's definitely more detailed."

"Do you think we'll find a clue inside this one, too? Look for a bed! The clue is usually behind the bed," Kate said.

Luke shone his flashlight into the hole in the building's roof, while Kate peered inside. "It's pretty empty in here, except for a lot of dirt," she said. "Wait, I think I see something in the back." She reached in. "It's another flat stone!"

Luke focused the light on the object in Kate's hand, with handwriting similar to the other two stones they had discovered. She read:

"*The next house and owner travel together,*
Never parting—no matter the weather.
Inside this home you will find a treasure
Whose value you won't be able to measure.

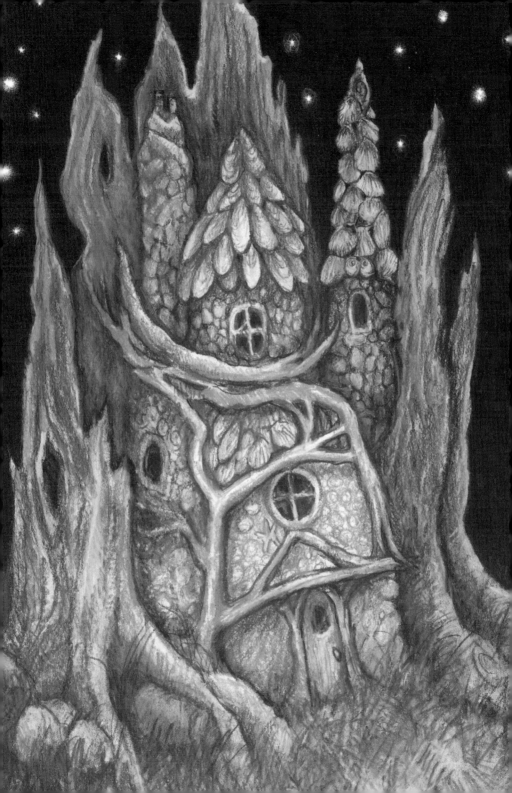

So many memories you will uncover
When this final prize you discover."

"Are these clues getting harder, or is it my imagination?" Luke sighed and checked his watch. "Uh-oh! It's almost nine o'clock. I have to be home!"

"We have to go back to my fairy house first," said Kate. "I left a letter for Mrs. Lennox there. I want to put your pictures in the envelope and leave it at her door."

Chapter
FOURTEEN

"Are you crazy? We can't go to Mrs. Lennox's house," Luke said.

"We have to! We need to tell her about the fairy houses. Come on." Kate pulled his arm. "We'll just slip it in her door."

"You don't know Mrs. Lennox," Luke said. "She'll be really mad if she catches us! Besides, that house is creepy, especially at night!"

"Fine, I'll go by myself," Kate said. "We have to tell her there is a mystery waiting to be solved in these woods. And if she sees these pictures, maybe she'll know what they mean."

Luke closed his eyes and took a deep breath. "Okay, I'll go. But, there's going to be trouble."

"It'll be worth it!" Kate beamed.

The two friends headed back on the moonlit path in silence. As they approached the rock where Kate had left the envelope, the hoot from a Great Horned Owl pierced the night air.

"That's a sign," Kate whispered. "That owl is asking us to help save its home."

"I think it's telling us to **go** home!" Luke said.

As they made their way toward Mrs. Lennox's house, they could see the porch light glowing in the distance. It reminded Luke of a lighthouse, but the beams from a lighthouse are meant to steer sailors away from danger, not toward it. But he said nothing.

They crept quietly across the lawn. Luke caught his breath when his flashlight revealed a big mouth! It belonged to one of the life-sized stone lions that guarded the walkway. Luke looked up at the massive porch. It covered the entire side of the house. The door and stairway were illuminated, but one corner of the porch was cloaked in darkness. Kate flinched as a bat dove at her from the roof. She shoved Luke from behind and they both crept up the granite steps. Luke slowly opened the screen door. Then Kate propped the envelope against the door inside.

"**What** are you two up to?" boomed a voice from the dark corner.

Luke whirled around, letting go of the screen door. Kate yelped as it smacked her in the shoulder. They turned in the direction of the voice. Mrs. Lennox emerged from the shadows

where she had been sitting all along. "Are you the **vandals** who paid me a visit the other night? Are you the ones who **destroyed** my flower beds and spray-painted my fence?"

Kate stepped forward to answer, but Mrs. Lennox continued in a stern voice. "You should both be ashamed of yourselves trying to frighten me like that." She glared at Luke and her eyebrows shot up in recognition. "Especially you, young fellow! You are supposed to be **caring** for my gardens, not destroying them!"

"We only wanted to give you this note," Kate said bravely, pointing to the envelope.

"And you!" She turned her anger to Kate. "Aren't you the girl who lives in my cottage? Does your mother know you're out this late?"

"But—" said Kate.

"Go home right now!" Mrs. Lennox said. "I will deal with this matter tomorrow, with your parents."

They bolted down the steps and across the lawn. "I told you so," Luke whispered as he headed toward his street. Kate started off in the opposite direction toward the cottage. But she looked back at the porch just long enough to see Mrs. Lennox pick up the envelope. With a satisfied nod, Kate headed for home.

Chapter FIFTEEN

Luke woke up Saturday morning with a start. He hoped Mrs. Lennox hadn't called his parents yet. When she did call, he would have a lot of explaining to do. He had to see Kate. They needed to figure out what to say to their parents. They also had to solve that last clue. The words played over in his mind as he headed downstairs. *House and owner travel together, never parting, no matter the weather.*

"Good morning," his dad said from behind his newspaper.

"Morning, Dad. Can I go over to Kate's this morning?"

"Not so fast, Buddy!" Mr. Carver said.

"What?" Luke worried Mrs. Lennox had called and he hadn't heard the ring.

"You have an errand to run for me," his dad said. Luke sighed with relief.

"I need you to take the skiff and pick up some lobster pots on the work float." The float was moored in the middle of a small cove on the Creek. It was used as a platform for repairing and storing lobster pots. Seagulls loved to rest there, which meant that its surface was mostly covered with seagull poop.

"Can Kate come with me?" Luke asked.

"Sure," his dad replied. "Make sure you have an extra life jacket for her."

"Okay," Luke raced to the phone. He figured the faster he got out of the house, the better.

As soon as Kate answered the phone, Luke asked, "Has Mrs. Lennox called your mom yet?"

"Not yet," she replied. "How about your parents?"

"No," he said. "But I think you should come over so we can make a plan."

Kate arrived a few minutes later and they immediately hopped in the skiff.

"When Mrs. Lennox reads our letter and sees the photos, she'll understand that we didn't wreck her gardens," Kate yelled over the roar of the motor.

A look of panic crossed Luke's face.

"What?" Kate asked.

"What if she doesn't believe us, Kate? What

if she thinks we were the ones? She might decide we can never go on her property again."

"Then we'd better sneak back to the woods this afternoon," Kate insisted. "It may be our only chance to figure out the last clue."

Luke maneuvered the skiff toward the center of the small cove, where the float was moored.

They noticed a mallard duck squawking and flapping its wings on the float. His cry was so loud they could hear it over the sound of the motor. The duck took off as their boat approached.

"Luke, something is wrong with that duck," said Kate.

Luke cut the motor. The duck landed in the water nearby, circling and quacking.

"Look!" Kate pointed to the stack of lobster pots. "There's something moving over there."

"It's another duck. That's the female!" Luke steered the skiff alongside and tied up to the float. "She's caught in the pot's netting. I bet that other duck is her mate. It looks like she's been struggling a long time. Let's try to get her out."

They worked together to open the top of the lobster pot. The duck was frantic, but they finally got her loose. The duck burst out of the netting, flying off toward shore, followed by her green-headed mate.

"We freed her, Sherlock!" Kate said.

"Well done, Watson, but we still have a clue to solve back on land," Luke reminded her with a grin. "Let's get going."

They loaded several pots into the skiff and headed back to shore, unaware that they were being watched by someone in the distance.

Chapter SIXTEEN

The two detectives planned to meet right after lunch by the stone fairy house they had discovered in the stump the night before. Luke rushed up the path and nearly plowed head first into Kate.

"I've been waiting for you!" Kate said. "What took you so long?"

"My mom told me I had to help Meg clean her room," huffed Luke. "Anyway, I've been thinking about that last clue. Maybe we should be looking somewhere else besides the woods. The clue says "house and owner travel together", so it can't be at the base of a tree."

"I was thinking the same thing! Look at this picture I found. Maybe this will help us!" Kate held out the copy of the photo from her mother.

"These kids are dressed like fairies! Are they relatives of yours?" Luke asked. "Are fairies part of your family history?"

Kate rolled her eyes. "It's Mrs. Lennox's mom with her aunt and uncle. They sometimes pretended they were fairies and had all kinds of adventures in these woods. About a hundred years ago. Isn't that weird?"

"Are you thinking they have something to do with figuring out the last clue?" asked Luke.

"I just have a feeling they're connected somehow. What if they built the houses and left the clues?"

Suddenly a sharp voice cut through the air. "What are you two up to now?"

They spun around and came face to face with Mrs. Lennox. She towered over them, with her arms crossed over her chest. Her face was covered with a scowl, her brow furrowed above piercing eyes.

"I've been watching you. I followed you to see what you are doing in my woods," Mrs. Lennox declared.

Luke stood as still as a statue.

Kate took a step forward. "H . . . h . . . hello, Mrs. Lennox."

"I saw you earlier on your boat," the woman said.

Luke's mouth hung open.

"We were—" Kate said.

"What were you doing with that duck?" Mrs. Lennox demanded.

"We tried—" Kate started.

"She and her mate have a nest on my shore," Mrs. Lennox interrupted. "I watched them build it. She'll be laying her eggs soon."

"She was stuck in a lobster pot! We had to get her out!" Luke blurted.

"Oh," Mrs. Lennox said, raising her eyebrows.

Kate took a deep breath. Luke's sudden outburst gave her the courage to take another step forward. "Mrs. Lennox, did you read our letter?"

"Yes," she answered. "What is the mystery you wrote to me about?"

"Do you know anything about this picture?" She handed the photograph of the three children to Mrs. Lennox. The elderly woman took a closer look. Her face softened as she gazed at the image.

"Oh, my goodness! This is my mother." She pointed to the older girl. "And my aunt and uncle." A smile spread across Mrs. Lennox's face. "Those three spent their summers in the Whitcomb Mansion on the point over there. They got into all sorts of mischief around this area. One time they tied a goat up to a cart and paraded into Portsmouth, pretending they were royalty! They even looked for buried treasure left by pirates on that island." Mrs. Lennox pointed to Clam Pit Island in the distance.

"Why are they dressed like fairies?" Kate asked.

"That was one of their favorite things to do," remembered Mrs. Lennox.

Kate and Luke looked at each other, their eyes wide. Fairies! "Mrs. Lennox, did you look at the pictures we sent you?"

"Yes," she replied. "But I couldn't make them out. What are they?"

"Will you come for a walk with us?" asked Kate. "We want to show you something."

Kate led her to the stone house. "Luke and I discovered this last night. That's what we've been up to, finding hidden fairy and gnome houses!"

Mrs. Lennox approached the sturdy structure. She bent down to get a closer look and gasped. "This is the fairy house my mother built. I can't believe it's still here!"

"It really is old then," said Luke.

"I suppose it is," smiled Mrs. Lennox. "My mother and her siblings played here. They called this place 'Fairyland.' I did, too, as a child. This is where the pond used to be."

"Pond?" Luke said. "There's no pond here!"

"Not now," Mrs. Lennox admitted. "But long ago the stream was damned up to create a small fish pond. Over the years, Mother Nature changed it back into a stream." She paused to look around. "I remember now. The pond had lily pads and beautiful large goldfish in it. But my favorite part was the fountain. It was a bronze sculpture of a turtle that spouted water from its mouth."

"Did you say turtle?" Luke interrupted. "House and owner travel together. That's it, Kate! We should be looking for a turtle! Where was it, Mrs. Lennox?"

"I think it was in this direction." Mrs. Lennox walked toward the stream, gesturing here and there, as she tried to picture how the pond used to look. Luke followed behind, mumbling that it had to be around here somewhere.

He shouted when he spotted an oval hump covered with moss. It looked like a boulder at first. Kate raced to join Luke. They began working together, stripping the moss until they revealed the shell of a large bronze turtle. Soon a head with an odd smile and wise old eyes peered up at them.

Mrs. Lennox came over and fiddled for a while with the underside of the shell, searching for something. Suddenly, the top squeaked and sprang open to reveal a hidden compartment.

Luke peeked inside. An old painted metal box was wedged next to the pipe that had once carried the water through the turtle and out its mouth. He carefully lifted it out and handed it to Mrs. Lennox. She tugged on the lid, but the hinge was rusted. When she yanked it, the lid flew off, spilling the contents onto the mossy floor. A few pieces of yellowed paper drifted down to rest at Mrs. Lennox's feet.

Mrs. Lennox picked them up. A look of surprise crossed her face as she recognized her own handwriting. She started to read softly,

"Best friends we are and will always be
Even when parted by the sea.
This private treasure is just our way
To mark this wonderful place to play.
These woods with Nature's help will keep
Our enchanted houses in magical sleep."

She slowly turned the other paper over and discovered a black and white photo, old and yellowed with cracks running through it. It was a picture of two children, a boy smiling with a pointy hat, holding hands with a girl dressed in a fairy costume.

Chapter
SEVENTEEN

"This was me," Mrs. Lennox exclaimed. "And this was my best friend Carl. He was a childhood friend from a long time ago." She showed Kate and Luke the photo. "I remember now. It was my twelfth birthday and I had a costume party. I was a fairy and Carl dressed up as a gnome. Everyone else came as cowboys or Indians, which was more fashionable at the time."

"Did you and Carl build the gnome and fairy houses?" Kate asked. "The ones in the pictures we sent you?"

"Yes! Now I know what your pictures are," Mrs. Lennox said. "Carl built the gnome home you found. He was from Sweden, where gnomes were popular. And I built the tooth fairy house. It all started when we discovered the large stone fairy house built by my mother when she was young, the one you just showed me. After that, these woods became our secret place and we spent hours exploring every inch of it."

"You and Carl must have left the clues we found!" Kate added.

"We did. It was silly, really. Creating a treasure hunt for ourselves," she said. "It was Carl's idea. He wanted to do something to cheer me up because he and his family were moving back to Sweden."

"What a great idea," Luke said, looking at Mrs. Lennox in admiration.

"Together we made a terrific team," she said. "After we wrote the clues on the stones, we carefully sealed up each one of the houses and then left the last clue in the turtle."

"Did you two forget about the fairy houses? You never uncovered the clues," Kate said.

Mrs. Lennox looked at Kate with somber blue eyes. "After Carl left, I wrote him every week for two months, but I never received a letter back. I was so hurt and angry. I decided not to have anything to do with our woods again. It was just after my thirteenth birthday that I finally received a letter."

"So he did write!" exclaimed Luke.

"No," Mrs. Lennox said sadly. "The letter was from his parents. After they had returned to Sweden, Carl became very ill."

"Did he die?" Kate asked.

"Yes," Mrs. Lennox lowered her head.

Kate placed her hand on Mrs. Lennox's arm. "It's hard to lose someone you think should be there for you in the future."

"I pretended that Carl had never existed." She looked around at the sunlight's streaks and shadows across the forest floor. The cool breeze brought a strong scent of pine as the leaves whispered softly. Then she continued. "It was just easier to forget about Carl and our secrets in the forest."

Mrs. Lennox looked at the photo of Carl. A Monarch butterfly fluttered by and landed on the corner of the image.

"The animals really seem to like these woods." Luke watched the butterfly's wings open and close as it rested next to the girl in the fairy costume.

"It's like you can feel the magic," Kate spoke softly, "and maybe that's why children have built fairy houses here."

Mrs. Lennox smiled as the butterfly took off and headed toward the stream. "This place is special, a treasure in fact, full of enchantment."

She began to pace on the path, her eyes looking at the photo in her hand and then up at the magnificent beauty around her. "Carl would have been so pleased to know his craftsmanship had withstood the test of time. He hoped to become an architect." She took a deep breath. "I have to figure out what to do with this land. Maybe I need some assistance," she said, thinking out loud.

"I'll help," Kate spoke up.

"Me too," added Luke.

Mrs. Lennox turned to the two hopeful faces looking up at her. Suddenly she felt like the young girl in the photo.

"Wonderful." Mrs. Lennox laughed and clapped her hands together. "Let's head back to the house. We have a lot to do!"

Chapter EIGHTEEN

"I am not going to see my land turned into condos and a shopping mall!" Mrs. Lennox handed glasses of lemonade to Luke and Kate, and then sat in her favorite rocking chair on the large porch. "Kate, maybe your mom could be on our team with all her knowledge about historic places."

"Uncle Rick knows about gardens," Luke offered.

"You're right!" said Mrs. Lennox. "We have to have Rick on the team. Let's start by giving the woods a name."

"How about 'The Forest of Natural Magic?'" said Luke.

"I was thinking of something more like 'Fairy Forest,'" Kate replied.

"They both have possibilities." Mrs. Lennox smiled. "And I like possibilities!"

Gravel crunched in the driveway. They all looked up to see Uncle Rick's truck pull into the courtyard.

"You're just in time, Rick," said Mrs. Lennox as he climbed the steps to the porch. "Sit down and have a glass of lemonade while we tell you about the mystery we've just solved."

"What are you two doing here?" Uncle Rick looked from Luke to Kate. "Is this about who's been vandalizing your gardens?"

"No. I wasn't even thinking about that!" Mrs. Lennox replied. "The mystery of the fairy houses in the enchanted forest! Luke and Kate discovered them in my woods."

"Fairy houses? What are those?" Uncle Rick inquired.

Luke told him the whole story.

"Watching Kate and your nephew today reminded me of how much fun I had in these woods as a child," Mrs. Lennox said.

"That's amazing," Uncle Rick said. "Generations of children playing, exploring and discovering, all on this property."

"I know!" Mrs. Lennox exclaimed. "This land is special to so many people. The forest is magic, I tell you. So we need to save it somehow.

We cannot allow it to be developed into a fancy hotel. What should I do?"

"What about preserving it?" Uncle Rick said. "It would be possible to keep the land as it is, so that people can enjoy it for generations in its natural state. There are many ways to do that."

"That would protect the wildlife, too," Luke said.

Just then, a bird flew inside the porch and darted into a corner of the roof.

"Speaking of wildlife," laughed Mrs. Lennox. "That phoebe and her mate have been nesting under the eaves of my porch for years. Wouldn't it be fitting to protect this land for the animals that live here?"

"That would be perfect," answered Kate.

"And to protect it for the children." Mrs. Lennox smiled. "So generations can keep visiting my woods to explore nature and build fairy houses."

Luke and Kate glanced at one another. Their eyes twinkled as if to say 'we did it!'

Chapter
NINETEEN

Luke entered the woods with a satisfied grin. Just yesterday he and Kate had met Mrs. Lennox and discovered the last clue.

He walked along the path that led to Kate's fairy house, carrying some clam shells and garden clippings that he and Meg had collected that morning. They were going to surprise Meg and show her the fairy houses now that the secret was out. He planned to fix up the house that Trevor tried to destroy, thinking it would please Kate. But as he rounded the bend, he saw Trevor crouching over the charred structure.

"What are you doing here?" Luke demanded. He hadn't seen Trevor since the night Trevor tried to burn down Kate's fairy house.

Trevor jumped up. "Nothing."

"What are you hiding behind your back?" Luke's eyes narrowed.

"None of your business!" Trevor said.

"Trevor!" Luke took a step forward.

"Here!" he yelled. He thrust a shell toward

his friend. It was shaped like a clam shell, but much larger. The inside was shiny with swirls of purples, blues and pinks.

"Is this the abalone shell you got from your mom? The one you always had on your dresser?" whispered Luke.

"I wanted to do something to fix this thing up before I leave tomorrow," he said.

"Want some help?" Luke asked. This was the Trevor he used to know.

"Fine," Trevor said.

Luke helped Trevor straighten out the sticks and take off the mud that made the teepee shape. Together they gently lifted the remaining charred sticks off the moss. They arranged the shell outside the structure, filling it with water from the nearby stream.

"Remember when we made boats together out of marsh reeds and raced them?" asked Luke.

"Yes," said Trevor, almost smiling. "Mine usually won."

"No, way," said Luke. "Let's make some now and see who wins."

"Next time," Trevor said. "I've got to get back. Don't tell Kate I was here, okay?"

"Why not?" Luke asked.

Trevor shrugged. "I just don't want her to know."

"Sure," Luke said.

"I'll see ya'." Trevor walked a few steps and turned back toward Luke. "Tell Mrs. Lennox I'm sorry about her garden."

"Okay," said Luke. He watched his friend disappear down the forest path.

Chapter TWENTY

"I can't believe school starts on Monday." Luke added more stones to the bridge he was building. He and Kate had dug a moat around their fairy castle. They had been working on the castle every day for the past two months. During that time, Mrs. Lennox had already formed a committee to help donate her property to the town.

"These flags should catch a fairy's attention," Kate said, adding three seagull feathers to the castle towers. "I can't wait to show this to Mrs. Lennox."

"I'm going to line up these pinecones and build a wall around the moat." Luke started gathering them from the ground.

The pinecones reminded Kate of Trevor. She had never told Luke about the time Trevor got chased by those bees. In a way, she was relieved that Trevor was gone, but she still felt sorry for him. "Have you heard from Trevor since he moved to Baltimore with his mom?"

"No," Luke replied as he put another pinecone in place. He smiled, remembering the shell that had mysteriously appeared at Kate's fairy house. "I sent him an e-mail, but no reply so far. I have a feeling that he'll be fine."

"Maybe he's nervous about starting at a new school and not knowing anyone. I know I am," Kate admitted.

"But you know me," Luke said. "I'll be in your class. Uncle Rick said the school was lucky to be getting a kid like you."

"He said that?" Kate adjusted one of the feathers on top of the castle. "You're lucky to have such a nice uncle. Anyone who takes so much time caring for a wild rabbit—"

"**Rabbit?**" Luke blurted out, dropping a pinecone.

"Yes, the one he caught in a trap at the park."

"Peter Rabbit?" Luke said.

"It's not Peter anymore. He changed her name to Petunia."

"**Her** name?" asked Luke.

"Your uncle caught the rabbit last week and put the trap in his shed. He planned to take it across the river into Maine the next morning and let it go. But when he picked up the trap, he discovered that the name Peter didn't fit, because she had given birth to three bunnies. Uh-oh," Kate stopped. "I forgot . . . I wasn't supposed to tell you."

"Peter had bunnies?" Luke asked. "What did Uncle Rick do with them?"

"Oh well, I may as well tell you the rest now," sighed Kate, putting down the sticks she was using to make a staircase. "He made a temporary home for them out of some lobster pots in his shed."

"Lobster pots!" Luke threw a stone at the dirt.

"He plans to make a shelter for them in the meadow on Mrs. Lennox's land by the Creek," Kate answered.

"Sagamore Creek?" Luke repeated.

Kate looked worried. "It was supposed to be a surprise! Rick was going to tell you tonight. He wants us to help him make the shelter tomorrow, and Mom is packing a picnic lunch."

"Those were all my ideas," Luke said.

"Using the lobster pots for a rabbit cage, letting it loose at Sagamore Creek."

"Your ideas?" Kate's eyes widened.

"Yeah, my ideas! I guess they inspired Uncle Rick." Luke leaned over and tapped Kate on the shoulder. "Race ya'!"

"Where to?" Kate leapt to her feet.

"To Uncle Rick's house, of course." Luke took off down the woodland path. "To see the rabbits!"

Tracy Kane

Tracy Kane is the author and illustrator of the award winning Fairy Houses Series® of books and video.

Inspiration for the Series came when visiting an island off the coast of Maine. There she discovered small natural habitats hidden in the woods. What a great idea and activity to share with children . . . everywhere! And that was the magical moment that led to her first book, *Fairy Houses.*

Tracy and her husband, Barry, have combined their talents and produced several enchanting books based on creating fairy houses. One of their favorite activities is exploring the natural wonders along the New England coast in their Zodiac boat.

When not on the water dodging lobster pot buoys, they are working at their home in New Hampshire.

Kelly Sanders

Kelly Sanders lives with her two daughters in Unionville, Connecticut. She is a Literacy Specialist in the Farmington Public School System, where she coaches teachers and teaches reading and writing to students in kindergarten through fourth grade. Kelly and her daughters are avid readers and writers.

Kelly loves going for long walks in the woods with her daughters and their dog, Shannon. Sometimes their cat, Perdy, follows along. They build fairy houses wherever they go, but their favorite spots are in Belfast, Maine, and Portsmouth, New Hampshire. Their fairy houses have been featured at Portsmouth's annual Fairy House Tour and Nature's Open House at Winding Trails in Farmington, Connecticut.